D1608883

Words to Know Before You Read

delicious

different

eggnog

kitchen

liquid

poached

solid

www.rourkeeducationalmedia.com

Edited by Precious McKenzie
Illustrated by Helen Poole
Art Direction and Page Layout by Renee Brady

Library of Congress PCN Data

Humpty Dumpty / Meg Greve
ISBN 978-1-61810-180-8 (hard cover) (alk. paper)
ISBN 978-1-61810-313-0 (soft cover)
Library of Congress Control Number: 2012936781

Rourke Educational Media
Printed in the United States of America,
North Mankato, Minnesota

rourkeeducationalmedia.com

customerservice@rourkeeducationalmedia.com • PO Box 643328 Vero Beach, Florida 32964

Humpty Dumpty

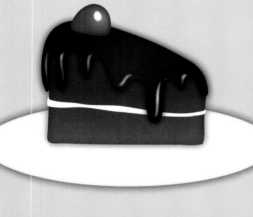

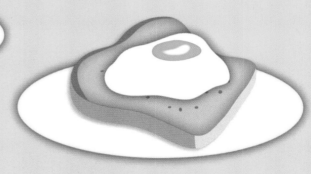

By Meg Greve

Illustrated by Helen Poole

Humpty Dumpty and his pals were eating breakfast in the king's kitchen.

Suddenly, someone bumped his pal.
He rolled right off his chair!

All the king's cooks and all the king's men couldn't put Humpty's pal together again!

So they made eggnog instead.

9

Humpty and his pals were eating lunch in the king's kitchen.

Suddenly, someone bumped his pal. She rolled off her chair!

All the king's cooks and all the king's men couldn't put Humpty's pal together again!

So they made a chocolate cake instead.

Humpty and his pal were eating dinner in the king's kitchen.

Suddenly, someone bumped his pal. He rolled off his chair!

All the king's cooks and all the king's men couldn't put Humpty's pal together again!

So they poached him instead.

17

Even though Humpty's pals changed,
they were still the same good eggs.

19

Humpty lived happily ever after because he decided it might be safer to eat in a different kitchen.

After Reading Activities

You and the Story...

Where did Humpty and his pals eat their meals?

Eggnog is a liquid. Can you name other liquids? What is special about a liquid?

Why did Humpty live happily ever after?

Words You Know Now...

Sort the words below into adjectives and nouns. Use each word in a sentence to retell the story.

delicious   liquid
different   poached
eggnog   solid
kitchen

You Could...Make Scrambled Eggs!

Be sure to ask for an adult's help

You Will Need:

- 2 eggs
- 2 tablespoons of milk
- a sprinkle of shredded cheese
- a bowl
- a whisk or fork
- a pan
- cooking spray
- salt and pepper

What To Do:

1. Crack both eggs into a bowl. Whisk the eggs until the yolks and the whites are mixed together.
2. Whisk in the milk.
3. Spray the bottom of a pan with cooking spray. Ask your adult to heat the pan.
4. Pour in the egg mixture and start to stir. When the eggs begin to harden, sprinkle the cheese over them and stir again.
5. Once the eggs are scrambled the way you like them, serve them on a plate. Season with a little bit of salt and pepper. (Do you like to eat your eggs with toast?)

About the Author

Meg Greve lives in Chicago with her husband, daughter, and son. Her daughter likes her eggs in a tortilla and her son likes his with ketchup.

Ask The Author!
www.rem4students.com

About the Illustrator

Helen Poole lives in Liverpool, England, with her fiancé. Over the past ten years she has worked as a designer and illustrator on books, toys, and games for many stores and publishers worldwide. Her favorite part of illustrating is character development. She loves creating fun, whimsical worlds with bright, vibrant colors. She gets her inspiration from everyday life and has her sketchbook with her at all times as inspiration often strikes in the unlikeliest of places!